THE
ELF
FLUTE

Kane Miller
A DIVISION OF EDC PUBLISHING

Kane Miller, A Division of EDC Publishing

Text © Anna Branford 2015
Illustrations © 2015 Lisa Coutts
Cover and internal design copyright © Walker Books Australia

For information contact:
Kane Miller, A Division of EDC Publishing
PO Box 470663
Tulsa, OK 74147-0663
www.kanemiller.com
www.edcpub.com
www.usbornebooksandmore.com

Library of Congress Control Number: 2015957641
Printed and bound in the United States of America
1 2 3 4 5 6 7 8 9 10
ISBN: 978-1-61067-532-1

THE
ELF
FLUTE

Lily
the Elf

Anna
Branford

Illustrated by Lisa Coutts

Chapter one

Lily lives with her dad
in a tiny elf house,
hidden under a bridge
in a busy city.

In the moss garden behind the house there is an even tinier house called a granny flat. And in the granny flat lives Lily's granny.

Lily is in the kitchen reading aloud one of her poems. She is planning to read it at the Grand Elf Concert tomorrow.

Just then, the mail bee arrives. Usually, he only brings ordinary letters. But this morning he has something special for Lily.

He hands her a long, thin package. Lily loves getting surprise packages. (She hops up and down with excitement.)

Dad helps Lily to undo the string. She tears open the brown paper.

Inside is a note and something wrapped in tissue.

The note says:

Dear Lily,

I was tidying my house today and I found this. I thought you might like to try it!

Love from Aunt Daisy

Aunt Daisy lives under another bridge a long way away. It is extra, extra exciting to get a present from far away. (Lily hops a bit more.)

She unwraps it very carefully. Suddenly, there is a flash of silver.

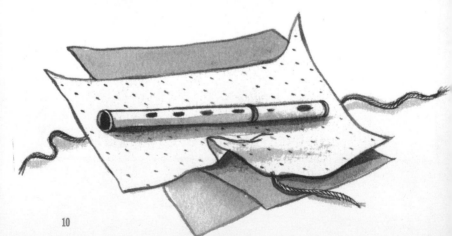

"An elf flute!" squeals Lily.

"It's a real beauty," says Granny.

Lily puts her poem away. It will be much more fun to play her new flute at the Grand Elf Concert. She is sure it will be very easy.

Chapter two

Lily has seen elf flutes
played at elf concerts
before. She knows
exactly what to do.

First, she holds the flute sideways. Next, she wiggles her fingers over the holes. Then she blows over the big hole at the top.

She waits for lovely music to fill the room. But there is only a whiffling sound.

Lily tries again. There is more whiffling.

"It might take a bit of practice," says Dad.

"I don't mind," says Lily. "The Grand

Elf Concert isn't until tomorrow. There's plenty of time." (Lily likes practicing.)

Lily takes the flute into her bedroom and practices all morning. She tries blowing very hard. The whiffling gets louder. Then she tries blowing very softly. The whiffling gets quieter.

It might be easier sitting
down, Lily thinks.

Then she tries lying
on her bed.

Then she tries dangling
upside down off her bed.

No matter what she tries,
there is still no lovely
music. Only whiffling.

Lily wonders if it might work better outside. There will be more air to blow in the moss garden.

She practices all afternoon. She tries standing in the breeze. She even tries standing on one foot on a toadstool. But it is no good.

Granny looks out of her window.

"What's that funny whiffling noise?" she asks.

"It's me," says Lily. "I want to play my new elf flute for the concert. But it is much, much harder than I thought."

Lily lets out a big deep sigh.

Chapter three

Dad comes outside to
do some gardening.

"Can I try your flute?"
he asks.

"Sure," says Lily. She is glad to have a break.

Dad makes a lovely sound like a bellbird.

Lily frowns. "Have you played an elf flute before?" she asks.

"It's my first time!" says Dad. "Must be beginner's luck."

He makes three more perfect bellbird sounds. Lily frowns even more.

"That sounded lovely," says Granny, coming out to see. "Can I try?"

"Okay," says Lily.

(She is too busy frowning to practice anyway.)

Granny picks up the flute. Right away, she plays a tune like a songbird singing.

Lily frowns much, much more.

"That was beautiful!" says Dad.

Everyone can play the elf flute except her.

Granny gives Lily back
her flute.

"I'd like to be on my
own for a while," says Lily.
She stomps back to her
bedroom with the flute.

Lily lies on her bed and sniffles into her pillow. Then she picks up her notebook. "I suppose I'll have to read my poem after all," she says to herself.

After some more
sniffling, she reads:

The Wind
Wild and strong
All night long
In the stormy weather
Soft and warming
In the morning
Lighter than a feather.

"Silly old poem,"
says Lily. She slams the
notebook shut.

Chapter four

In the evening after
dinner everyone practices
their concert act. Dad
plays an elf tune on his

fiddle. Lily and Granny clap for him. Granny sings a very old song about forgotten elf magic. Lily and Dad clap for her. Then it is Lily's turn.

Lily reads her poem. Dad and Granny listen carefully. Then they both clap for a long time.

"It's perfect for the concert," says Dad.

"Beautiful!" agrees Granny. "The elves are going to love it."

"I don't love it," says Lily in her best grumbling voice. "I wanted to play my new flute."

At bedtime, Granny tucks her in.

"I hope it's a windy night for the concert," says Lily.

"Why?" asks Granny.

"Real gusts of wind would make my poem sound more exciting," explains Lily. "It still won't be as good as elf flute music. But it would be better than a plain old poem."

"Maybe you could make the noise of the wind as you read," Granny suggests.

Granny makes lots of
funny whooshing noises to
show Lily what she means.
Lily tries not to giggle,
but she can't help it.

Later on, just as she is about to close her eyes, Lily looks over at the silver flute. It is on her dresser, twinkling in the moonlight.

Then, suddenly, Lily has a very good idea.

Chapter five

The next day everyone gets ready for the Grand Elf Concert. Dad polishes his fiddle and wears his

best hat. Granny does
special warm-up singing
and wears her sparkliest
brooch.

Lily brushes her hair
and makes her elf shoes
extra shiny.

She has tucked her poem
carefully in her pocket.
But before they leave for
the concert, she also slips
the elf flute into her bag.

"Might you need a
bit more practice?"
asks Dad, looking
worried.

"I don't think
so," says Lily.

"Are you
sure?" asks
Granny, looking
worried too.

"I'm sure,"
says Lily.

At the concert they watch the elves performing their acts on the stage. Some play trumpets, drums and guitars. Others do dancing, headstands and magic tricks. Soon it is their turn.

First, Granny sings her elf song. Everyone sings along.

Then Dad plays his tune on the fiddle. The elves tap their toes.

Finally, Lily walks onto the stage.

She takes her elf flute out of her bag. She holds it up and blows into it very hard. It makes a loud whiffling sound, like a wild wind. Dad and Granny look more worried than ever.

Then Lily reads the first part of her poem in her wildest, stormiest voice.

The Wind
Wild and strong
All night long
In the stormy weather

Lily lifts her flute again and blows very softly – just like a gentle breeze.

For the second part,
she uses her softest,
lightest voice.

Soft and warming
In the morning
Lighter than a feather.

The elves clap and cheer and make whooshing windy noises. With a big smile, Lily takes a bow. She played her elf flute perfectly!

Other
Lily the Elf
books by
Anna Branford

Lily the elf finds a
beautiful ring.

The midnight owl
sounds scary!

Dandelion seed wishes
always come true –
don't they?